PeeWee's Tale

PeeWee's Tale

Johanna Hurwitz

ILLUSTRATED BY
Patience Brewster

SeaStar Books
NEW YORK

First published in the United States by SEASTAR BOOKS,
a division of NORTH-SOUTH BOOKS, INC., New York.
Published simultaneously in Canada, Australia, and New Zealand by North-South Books,
an imprint of Nord-Süd Verlag AG, Gossau Zürich, Switzerland.

Library of Congress Cataloging-in-Publication Data is available.

The art for this book was prepared using pencil.
The text for this book was set in 16-point Centaur MT.

ISBN I-58717-027-2
I   3   5   7   9   TB   IO   8   6   4   2

Printed in the United States of America

For more information about our books, and the authors and artists who create them,
visit our web site: www.northsouth.com

This book is for
a teller of tales & good friend,
Barbara Ann Porte

—J. H.

CONTENTS

CHAPTER ONE

A Birthday Present

I was born in a cage in Casey's Pet Shop. Though my eyes were open, I can't remember my first hours or days. But soon I became aware of the wonderful smell of my mother and four siblings. We huddled together for warmth and comfort. I drank my mother's milk and scratched my tiny paws on the floor of the cage.

One by one, my brothers and sisters left

home to be adopted by humans. And by the time I was a few months old, I had a new home too. On May 2, I became the birthday present for a nine-year-old boy named Robbie Fischler. It didn't take long for me to discover that he'd been hoping for a dog.

"What's this peewee thing, Uncle Arthur?" he asked as he was handed my cage, which was tied with a red bow that was larger than me.

"Haven't you ever seen one, Robbie? It's a guinea pig," Uncle Arthur told him.

I stood up straight and proud as I looked at Robbie through the mesh wire of the cage.

"Guinea pigs are members of the rodent family, like mice," my new owner was told.

"Oh, Arthur! How could you bring such a disgusting creature into this apartment?" a woman complained loudly.

"Now, Barbara . . . Robbie is my only nephew and it's time he had a pet of his own to take care of."

"I wish it was a puppy," Robbie said gently. "I don't think guinea pigs can do anything."

I ran around inside my cage trying to act like a puppy. I'd seen many at Casey's Pet Shop. I couldn't bark or wag my tail, but I tried to look cute and friendly.

"Your parents would have had a fit if I walked in here with a dog," Uncle Arthur explained. "Besides, a guinea pig is so much easier to care for. It'll help you develop a sense of responsiblity for when you do get a dog."

"We have no plans of getting him a dog," Robbie's mother said. "Arthur, you should have asked me before you brought this rodent here."

Robbie opened the cage and put his hand inside to pick me up. Mrs. Fischler screamed and backed away as her son stroked my fur. I rubbed against Robbie the way I'd noticed cats doing in the pet shop. Maybe that would make my new owner happy.

It seemed to work.

"He's awfully cute," Robbie admitted, looking at my dark brown fur, which has streaks of reddish brown here and there. I also have a reddish-brown strip down the center of my face.

Robbie smiled. "I really, really like him. Thanks a lot, Uncle Arthur. I'll pretend he's a dog."

"And I'll pretend he isn't here," Robbie's mother said, shuddering.

When Robbie's father came home, I was shown proudly to him. "I'm going to call him PeeWee," Robbie announced. "Because he's so small."

"Hi, PeeWee," Mr. Fischler said to me.

"Why couldn't Arthur have given him some goldfish?" Mrs. Fischler asked her husband. "Instead he gave Robbie a *rodent*."

"Don't worry," Robbie's dad said. "He's in a cage. He won't bother you."

"But Arthur *knows* how I hate mice," Mrs. Fischler said. "I've hated them ever since we were children."

"PeeWee's not a mouse," Robbie reminded his mother.

"Come on. Let's get ready," Robbie's father said, trying to distract his wife. "Remember, we're taking Robbie out to dinner and to a movie to celebrate his birthday."

In a little while, I was alone in my cage in Robbie's bedroom. Unlike the pet shop, there were no other cages or animals around. But still, there was plenty for me to see. There were brightly colored curtains on the windows, a bed with a matching spread, and shelves filled with toys and books. I decided that Robbie's mother couldn't be all bad if she'd fixed up her son's room and given him so many toys.

My new cage was smaller than the one in which I lived at Casey's Pet Shop, but at least I didn't have to share it with any other guinea pigs. Just like before, the bottom of my cage was covered with scraps of paper. It would be Robbie's job to remove the scraps from time to time as they became dirty and wet. He would have to replace them with other scraps.

Back at Casey's, I had first noticed that there were markings on the papers. They were all different, black and strange. I looked at them closely.

When my mother saw my interest, she explained them to me. "Those are letters of the alphabet," she had told me. "There are twenty-six big and twenty-six small ones. Together the letters join to make words that humans can understand. They call it *reading*."

"How do you know about them?" I asked her.

That was when I learned that she had been born in a cage inside a schoolroom. "It was filled with boys and girls who were being taught the letters," she said. "I learned the entire alphabet faster than most of the children," she added proudly.

After that, I began to study the bits of paper. My brothers and sisters thought that I was weird to want to look at those scraps.

"They don't taste good," said one brother.

"You can't climb on them," said one of my sisters.

I didn't care what my brothers and sisters said. Every day, after I finished eating, I sifted through the paper bits. My mother taught me how to recognize the straight and curved lines that made up the letters. It wasn't easy, but after a while, I could tell them apart.

Soon I, like my mother, could read all the letters on the scraps. I read them aloud. *Ne* and *May* and *TI*.

"But what does it mean?" I asked my mother. "What's the point of learning these letters if they don't say something that makes sense?"

"Don't forget you're reading scraps," my mother reminded me. "The children in the schoolroom had books with whole pages of letters that told them fine stories. They didn't have the little bits and pieces that we have here."

I had looked down at the floor of the cage. Perhaps if I pushed the pieces together, I could create a whole page that would tell a story too. But it never worked. All I could read were more scraps that said *Opr* and *Yor* and *Majo*.

Now, in my new cage in Robbie Fischler's bedroom, I studied the scraps again. The pieces of paper in my new cage were just as small and meaningless as they had been in my old one though. If only they were larger! Still, seeing the books on the shelf in the room gave me hope. Perhaps I would finally have a chance to see one of them open with a complete page in front of me. Then I could read a story.

CHAPTER TWO

In the Dark

It didn't take me long to adjust to my new home. One cage is pretty much like another: four sides, a water supply, an exercise wheel. But belonging to Robbie was much more fun than living in the pet store. Because he really wanted a dog, Robbie treated me as if I were one. He didn't make me stay inside my cage. Instead, he often let me out to explore his bedroom. At first, I was a little timid. But soon I learned to run under his bed; I hid inside his bedroom slippers; I walked around inside the dark closet where his clothing hung.

Maybe it was because he didn't have any brothers or sisters, but Robbie talked to me a lot. Sometimes he held me up to the window. I could see the street below with the cars going along. And in the distance, I noticed a large area of green. "That's the park where I go and play with my friends," Robbie explained to me.

What was the park like? I wondered. But my world inside Robbie's apartment was big enough to keep me busy.

One day Robbie's mother walked into his bedroom. Robbie was sitting on his bed and I was on his lap while he gently combed my fur.

"What do you think you're doing?" Mrs. Fischler yelled.

"I'm combing PeeWee's hair. You're always telling me to comb mine," Robbie explained.

"Throw that comb into the garbage at once," his mother told him. "I don't want it to go anywhere near your head ever again. I'll get you a new comb, but it's just for you—*not* that rodent."

"If you're getting me a new comb, I can save this one for PeeWee," Robbie suggested.

"No! I don't like you handling him so much.

And I never want to see him on your bed either. Put him back in his cage where he belongs."

That was bad, but worse was to come. One day when Robbie let me out of my cage, I went into the hallway outside his bedroom. Just at that moment, Mrs. Fischler came walking by. She took one look at me and she let out a deafening shriek.

"Help!" she screamed so loudly that she frightened me. I ran around in a circle looking desperately for a place to hide.

Robbie came running.

In her panic, Mrs. Fischler had jumped up on a nearby chair.

"What is that creature doing out here?" she shouted.

"PeeWee was just taking a little walk," said Robbie picking me up.

"Lock him inside his cage immediately!" his mother called to Robbie. "And keep him in it."

So Robbie took me back into his room and placed me inside my cage.

"Isn't she silly?" Robbie whispered to me. "How could anyone be afraid of you, PeeWee?"

Even though I

wasn't hungry, I nibbled on one of the dry pellets that was the major part of my diet. Eating, drinking, and running on the exercise wheel were the only activities that I had. Of course, I still occasionally studied the letters on the scraps of paper on the floor of my cage. Even though they made no sense, I wanted to keep my ability to read.

So life at the Fischlers' continued, and I was careful not to leave Robbie's bedroom. I didn't want to frighten his mother and I really didn't want her to frighten *me*.

One evening when Robbie had a sleepover date at the home of one of his classmates, Mrs. Fischler came into his bedroom. Mr. Fischler was with her.

Lying quietly in a corner of my cage, I listened to Robbie's parents speaking together.

"Barbara, I don't like this at all," Mr. Fischler said to his wife. "He's going to be very upset when he comes home."

"Robbie didn't even want a guinea pig," Mrs. Fischler responded. "If my brother hadn't given it to him for his birthday, we wouldn't have this problem. But I can't go about my own home in fear that this thing is going to get out."

"What does it matter if he does? This poor guinea pig can't possibly hurt you."

"You don't understand," Mrs. Fischler said. "I keep imagining this rodent in every corner. I can't relax. I even wake at night thinking of him crawling around. We'll just tell Robbie that he got out of the cage and got lost. He'll feel bad for a day or two, but he'll get over it. And I'll make it up to him in some way."

"What you want to do is probably illegal," Mr. Fischler said.

I stood up in my cage. What were the Fischlers going to do? I wished Robbie was there to protect me.

Mr. Fischler opened my cage and took me out. "He is a handsome fellow," he said to his wife as he stroked my fur. "I'm only going along with this because I'm concerned about what the guinea pig is doing to your blood pressure."

I looked at Robbie's mother. What was blood pressure? I wondered. Mrs. Fischler nodded her head. "Go on already. Put him in the box and get him out of here," she said.

Robbie's father put me inside a small box. At once, the lid was placed on top of it and it became too dark for me to see anything.

"I'll be back in twenty minutes," I heard Mr. Fischler say.

After that, there were no more words. But the box jiggled up and down, and I guessed that Mr. Fischler was carrying me someplace. I ran around in the small space trying to find a way out. What was happening to me? I was sure it couldn't be good.

After a while, the motion of the box stopped. The lid was removed. Although it was only dimly lit, I could see the face of Robbie's father looking down at me.

"Well, good luck, PeeWee," he

said, stroking my fur gently. "It's not your fault that you were born a guinea pig."

Then he took me from the box and placed me down on the floor. It felt damp and prickly, not at all like the paper-covered floor of either of my cages or the soft carpeting at Robbie's home.

In the dim light, I could see the shoes and legs of Mr. Fischler begin to move away from me. I ran after him as fast as I could. But my legs are so very small and my feet are even smaller. Mr. Fischler got farther and farther away and soon I knew it was hopeless. I couldn't possibly catch up with him. I could hardly breathe from all my running and my mouth was dry with thirst.

When I finally started moving again, one of my paws stepped into something wet. I turned around and discovered a puddle of water. Nothing ever tasted so good as that cool liquid on my tongue.

Now I wasn't thirsty, but I was very, very tired. I was too tired to be afraid, too tired to wonder where I was. All I wanted was to curl up and take a nap. When I awoke, I would think about how I could find Robbie.

Near where I was standing, there was a small cage. I circled around and saw that it had only three walls. Still, I felt I would be safer inside it than out. In all my life, I'd never slept outside of a cage.

Inside, the cage had an unusual smell. I licked a small part of it and discovered a fine salty taste. So I licked one whole wall before I fell asleep.

CHAPTER THREE

A New World

I woke with a thud. Suddenly, I found myself rolling round and round. It took me a moment to realize that I was not inside the wheel or even inside my usual cage. I was someplace else.

Finally, my new home rolled to a halt. After my heart stopped thudding, I cautiously stepped outside. It was no longer dark like the night before, and now I could see many strange sights.

Color was all around me, more beautiful than the curtains and bedspread in Robbie's room. I marveled at brilliant yellow and a

hundred shades of green. I could hear many birds singing, and their songs were sweeter than those of the birds I'd known in the pet shop. Moving forward, I sniffed at the ground. This place smelled pretty wonderful too!

I ran to a nearby puddle and took a long drink. On my way, I noticed that the ground seemed to be in two parts. Some was covered with something hard, and the rest was softer and had plants growing from it. I nibbled one of the plants and discovered that the taste was much, much better than my old pellets.

"Who in the world are you?" a voice asked.

Startled, I looked around but I could see no one.

"Up here," said the voice. "In the tree."

I raised my head and noticed a tall structure, even taller than Robbie's father or his uncle

Arthur. At first I thought this tall thing was speaking to me. But then I noticed a small creature sitting on one of the many arms.

I had never seen such an animal before. He was close to my size and he was a dull gray color, except for his chest, which was white. He came closer to me with amazing speed.

That's when I became aware of the most incredible thing about him: his tail. My tail is a small useless stub, but his was long and full and waved back and forth as he moved. I had seen dog and cat tails in the pet shop, but none that were as magnificent as the one this creature had.

"I'm PeeWee," I told him when he landed on the ground beside me. "I'm a guinea pig. What are you?"

"I'm a squirrel," the creature said proudly as

he scratched himself with one of his rear legs. "My name is Lexington. But you can call me Lexi."

"Where are we?" I asked my new friend.

"We're near Seventy-third Street in the borough of Manhattan, which is in New York City," Lexi told me. "And I was named after one of its avenues. I have brothers named Amsterdam, Columbus, and Madison."

"I belong to a boy named Robbie," I explained to Lexi. "But I don't know where he is."

"It's better to travel alone," the squirrel replied. "I have many, many brothers and sisters and cousins, but I belong to no one. In fact, there are so many in my family that most just have numbers, like the streets of Manhattan. Sometimes we chatter to one another as we run up and down the trees. But we're all so busy looking for food and watching for dangers that we have no time for real conversation."

"Well, I'm glad you're talking to me," I said. "Robbie's father brought me here last night. But I need to find my way back home to Robbie. You haven't seen a young boy with spots on his face that are called freckles? He has a chipped front tooth too. He would have been looking for me."

"No," Lexi admitted. "But I'll climb to the top of my tree and take a look."

I watched him as he scampered up the structure that I now knew was called a tree. He ran so quickly jumping from branch to branch that I grew dizzy, and my eyes could scarcely follow his path.

"I see a boy with red hair," Lexi called down to me. "Does that sound like your Robbie?"

"Nope," I said. "Robbie's hair is dark brown."

"There's another boy walking a dog," Lexi reported as he came running down the tree toward me.

"That can't be Robbie. He doesn't have a dog." I sighed with disappointment.

"Well, here. Take this. Maybe it will cheer you up," Lexi said, dropping something from his mouth. It rested at my feet. "Don't ever say I never gave you anything."

"What is this?" I asked, looking at a round, hard object.

"Didn't you ever see a nut?" asked Lexi, scratching himself again. "They're delicious. I keep a big supply hidden inside a hole in this tree."

I moved closer to the object, but before I could attempt to eat it, Lexi stopped me. "Whatever you do, don't forget: *Look before you eat*. It's one of the first things my mother taught me," he said.

I looked around me and then licked the object, but there was no taste.

"Bite it. Break the shell," said Lexi. He seemed amazed at my stupidity, but of course, I'd never seen a nut before.

My teeth, which were strong enough to chew the little pellets Robbie gave me, couldn't pierce the shell.

"Look," Lexi instructed. He picked up the nut in his paws and almost immediately I could hear a cracking sound as his teeth made a hole in the hard shell.

"Now taste," he said.

I bit into the soft center of the nut and Lexi was right. It was delicious, but I didn't have much time to enjoy it.

"Watch out!" screeched Lexi suddenly, racing up the tree.

Coming toward me was an enormous dog. He ran faster than Lexi, and even from a distance, I could see that his teeth were very, very large.

"Climb the tree!" Lexi shouted down to me.

I scampered to the tree but my paws could not hold on to its rough surface. I scratched and scratched at the sides and finally got an inch off the ground. But right away, I slipped, and landed where I had begun.

The animal's barking grew louder and louder. It was almost upon me. I closed my eyes and waited for the worst.

CHAPTER FOUR

Lessons from Lexi

Just as I expected to find myself in the jaws of the terrible creature, nothing happened. I opened my eyes to see what was going on. Suddenly, the dog had turned to run in another direction. I shivered with relief as I wondered why he had lost his interest in me. And then I saw. It was all Lexi's doing.

My new friend had climbed down from his safe perch in the tree and set himself in the path of the huge dog. Lexi knew he could avoid being caught by the big animal. As soon as the dog was about to jump at him, Lexi charged off in a different direction. At once, the dog changed course. The dog was too dumb to realize that he would never be able to catch a creature who could run and climb and jump with squirrel speed. It was an amazing performance.

Before long, Lexi's game was interrupted by a human who came shouting and calling and waving a long strap.

"Figaro . . . Figaro . . . Figaro!" it called out, then shouted, "Heel!"

The animal stopped and looked at the human. He looked longingly at Lexi but he didn't try and catch him.

"Good dog," the voice encouraged.

I watched as the human connected the strap he was holding to a band around the dog's neck and pulled the dog away. I wish Robbie would come calling for me, I thought as Lexi came running toward me.

"*A leap in time is mighty fine,*" he said. "Why didn't you climb the tree?"

"I tried," I said. "But my legs are shorter than yours."

"I climbed trees when I was a baby, and my legs were guinea-pig size," Lexi responded.

"Perhaps it's because I haven't a tail," I said.

"My cousin Sixty-seven was hit by a car and lost his tail. He can still climb even without it. You just need lessons," Lexi retorted. "I'll teach you how to climb. *Practice makes perfect.*"

Somehow, I guessed that no number of lessons would ever give me the speed and climbing skills of a squirrel. But I was glad of my new friend's interest in me.

"You need a place to live too," said Lexi. "All the animals in the park have their own shelters."

"At Robbie's house, I live in a cage," I explained. That reminded me. Robbie was probably back home now, and he would be wondering where I had disappeared to.

"There's a zoo with cages here in the park," said Lexi. "But you're better off finding your own place to stay. Then you can come and go as you please. The zoo animals are locked up. It's better to have the freedom of the whole park."

I looked around me. So this was the park, I thought, suddenly realizing where I was. It was the piece of green that I'd seen so often from Robbie's window. The place where he came to play.

"What exactly is a park, anyhow?" I asked.

"It's all these trees and grass and flowers," Lexi explained. "It's those benches where people will be sitting before long, and these paths for them to walk along. It's the sky above us and the air around us. It's our whole world."

"I never knew the world could be a park," I told him. "I come from a much smaller world with a wheel and a door and pellets for food and paper scraps on the floor."

"Sounds awful," said Lexi.

"It wasn't awful," I told him. But I already knew that now I would find my old world very small. No wonder Robbie liked coming to the park to play with his friends.

"We'd better hurry," said Lexi. "Pretty soon there will be a lot of people around. There will be small children and their parents, park attendants, roller skates, and bicycles. And *many* more dogs. You need a place where you can escape. If you can't climb a tree, you'd better find a hole."

I looked down at the ground. It was soft and slightly damp under my paws. Without thinking, I began digging into it. Soon, I found myself deep inside a hole that I had made. I didn't even know that I could do such a thing.

"What do you think of this?" I called up to Lexi.

"Personally, I'd hate to be inside a dirty hole in the ground," he said. "A hole is a fine place for hiding nuts, but I wouldn't want to live there."

For a moment, I was sorry about Lexi's disapproval. But suddenly, I knew that if I could dig a hole, I'd always be safe—safe inside the burrow of Manhattan.

CHAPTER FIVE

A Picnic in the Park

I must have dozed off in my burrow. I woke feeling both thirsty and hungry. I poked my head out of the hole and saw many humans of all sizes walking nearby. I knew it would be dangerous for a guinea pig to go exploring among all those people. But the noise and activity filled me with excitement rather than fright. If only Robbie were with me, everything would have been perfect.

Cautiously, I climbed out of my hole and found my old puddle. It had become much smaller while I was asleep, but I was able to get a drink. Then I looked about for something to eat. I spotted a round object that had been chewed a bit already by some creature or other. The smell was sweet, so I took a nibble. It filled my mouth with a delicious juice, so I didn't get thirsty as I always did when I ate the pellets that Robbie fed me. There was no question—the park food was much more interesting than cage food.

Something whizzed by me that reminded me at once that I had to be careful. I dragged the food toward my burrow, where there seemed to be less activity.

"I see you woke up," a voice called out to me. It was my friend Lexi high above. I watched nervously as he jumped from branch to branch of his tree until he made it down to the ground beside me. It did make me dizzy to watch him.

"Have a bite of this," I offered when he reached me.

"Apples aren't bad," he said as he gnawed off a large chunk. "And this is a sweet one. Sometimes they are sour. I don't like sour. Do you know the old saying? *An apple a day keeps the aches away.* But if truth be told, nothing beats a good nut."

He chewed a bit more and then looked at me. "I wish human beings were as fond of nuts as I am. Wherever there are people, you can always find a good meal, because they leave so much garbage. They love to sit on the grass and have picnic meals. Then they drop bits of sandwiches, ice-cream sticks, paper cups, candy wrappers, newspapers, and whatever other junk they brought with them. I once overheard a park worker say that visitors to the park create fifteen thousand tons of garbage each day. I just wish it were fifteen thousand tons of nuts instead."

I took in this information and all the new words that Lexi kept using: apple, sandwich, garbage. There was so much for me to learn about here in the park. These were things I never even knew existed when I was with Robbie.

And that made me think of my owner. "Listen," I asked Lexi. "You haven't seen Robbie Fischler yet, have you?" I knew Robbie would be worried about me when he discovered that my cage was empty.

Lexi scratched himself and shook his head. "I did see a group of boys playing ball when I was up in the tree. But to tell you the truth, all the boys who come to this park look alike to me. I can't tell one from another."

I wished I could climb to the top of Lexi's tree and have a good look around. I would know Robbie the minute I saw him. Then I suddenly had a new thought. Perhaps if I ate nuts, the way Lexi did, I would grow a tail too. And with a tail, I could balance myself and climb up a tree. Then I could watch for Robbie. On the other paw, it might take too long waiting for my tail to grow.

"I'm going to have to travel about the park searching for Robbie," I explained to Lexi. "He's a great kid. He really wanted a puppy for his birthday. But once he got me, he was a good owner. I'm sure he's out hunting for me right this minute."

"Why would he think you're in the park?" Lexi asked.

"Where else would an animal go?" I asked him.

"Suit yourself, if you want to go looking," Lexi said. "But this park is pretty big. It has eight hundred and forty-three acres. I don't even have that many brothers and cousins."

I thought about what he'd told me. I didn't even know what an acre was. But from my knowledge of letters and numbers, I did know that eight hundred and forty-three was a very big number.

Lexi ran around in a circle and came back to me. "I have to warn you. The park can be very dangerous. You've only seen one dog in action. But there are things worse than dogs. Out on the roadway, big motor cars come with heavy wheels. I'm sorry to say that I've lost more than one of my relatives when they were flattened on the roadway."

He stopped speaking while he scratched himself. And then he continued. "Like I said before, you're better off just taking care of yourself and not worrying about others. Fill your own belly first. That's the law of nature."

I looked fondly at my new friend. He might pretend not to care about anyone but himself. But look what he'd done to help me. Already he had saved my life, taught me a bit about the new world around me, and he'd even given me a nut.

"I'll be extra careful," I promised Lexi. "Where did you see the children playing?"

"They were in the ball field near the lake." He pointed with his nose.

"I've got to go," I told him.

"Be careful you don't get caught," Lexi warned me again. "Everything in the park seems to move faster than you."

"I'll watch out," I told him as I started off. I felt a bit sad. I liked Lexi, and I knew that if I found Robbie, I'd return to my old cage and I'd never see my new friend again.

I tried to run with a confident step, but inside, I was quivering. Would I find Robbie? Or would something find me?

CHAPTER SIX

Words with a Warning

Because I had spent more time reading the paper scraps in my cage than using the exercise wheel, I wasn't very strong. I often had to stop and rest. Remembering Lexi's warning, I took care to hide myself behind stones or tree trunks. I discovered that I could squeeze myself into the small spaces where the trees grew out of the ground. I felt very safe resting in those cozy holes.

The best thing about my travels was that I could always find something good to eat whenever I felt a little hungry. I could nibble on some of the grasses or other plants that were growing wild all around me. I also found something that I couldn't identify, but that tasted especially delicious. It was made of three parts, one on top of the other. The outer sides were the same, but in the middle was something sweet combined with a taste that reminded me of the nut Lexi had given me.

While I was resting in one of the tree holes, a breeze brought a large piece of paper through the air. It landed nearby, and I was so excited to see such a large piece of paper with so many connected letters that I forgot myself and ran out into the open to investigate. For the first time in my life, I was seeing letters that formed real words. And suddenly I became very excited by the skill I knew I had. At last I would be able to read a complete story. I walked along the paper, sounding out the words and trying to learn their message:

YANKS BEAT RED SOX 7–4
IN 12-INNING GAME

I was able to read the words but they made no sense to me whatsoever. I crawled along the paper looking for another message to read.

METS SCORE HEAVILY
IN DOUBLEHEADER AGAINST BRAVES

It was another meaningless story. What was the point of knowing how to read if the story had nothing worthwhile to say?

I walked off the paper, disappointed. But at that moment, a breeze flipped another page of the paper into view. I looked again and this time I found a story that I could understand.

NEW PLAYGROUND PLANNED
FOR CENTRAL PARK

Within the next few days, construction will begin on a new play area for the city's children. Designed by Steven Zalben, this playground will have ingenious climbing structures and imaginative cubicles in which children can create hiding places and clubhouses for their games. The project has been funded by private money raised by The Friends of Central Park.

Only eight maple trees, at 73rd Street near

Fifth Avenue, will be affected by the construction. They will be cut down to make room for the play area. "We are always sorry to lose one of our trees," the park commissioner was quoted as saying at a press conference announcing the new playground. "But we know the play area will bring much joy to the city's children. And that, of course, is one of the primary goals of our park." The public is urged to keep out of the construction area until this project is completed.

My first thought was how much Robbie would enjoy climbing and playing there. But then I realized something terrible. Wasn't Lexi's tree near 73rd Street? Wouldn't his home be in danger now? What would happen to all the nuts that he stored there? Wouldn't his entire food supply be lost when they cut down his tree? I was about to turn back and warn Lexi that he was going to lose his home. But just at that moment, I heard the sound of shouting and cheering children playing nearby. I wanted to turn back, but at the same time, the voices of the children made me long for Robbie. And so I continued on, away from Lexi, toward the children.

CHAPTER SEVEN

I Meet a Group of Children

As I neared the children, I could hear their voices getting louder and louder. But soon a group of fat pigeons blocked my way. "Food, food," they mumbled as they pecked at the dirt. The pigeons were bigger than any of the birds I'd known at Casey's Pet Shop. They ate a lot more too. And unlike the parakeets at the pet shop, who could speak entire sentences, the pigeons had a very limited vocabulary.

They said the same word over and over. "Food. Food."

"I don't want your food," I shouted to them, although I was getting hungry and tired once again.

Finally, I could see the lake. It was like a huge shining water dish that could provide drink for every guinea pig in the world. In the play area, there were many children who were busy in a game of ball. Off in the distance, I could see Robbie running with the others. My heart beat fast with delight. As I rushed toward him, a breeze blowing the leaves sounded like cheers and applause.

"Hey, what's that?" one of the children called out.

"It's a rat!" shrieked one of them.

"No it's not. It's a guinea pig like we have at school."

Someone scooped me up and held me tightly. All of the other children came running to get a good look at me. I could see their faces better now. When I looked at the boy who I'd been sure was Robbie, I saw I was wrong. He was the same size and had dark hair, but he didn't have freckles. I know you can't wash freckles off, because Robbie had told me that one evening when he was talking to me.

"What should we do with him?" the boy who looked like Robbie asked.

The boy who was holding me squeezed me painfully. It had never hurt when Robbie held me.

I didn't wait for them to decide what they wanted to do with me. If Robbie had been there, it would have been different. But he wasn't, so I knew I had to get away. Without even thinking, I did something I'd never done before. I nipped the hand of the boy who was holding me.

"Ouch!" he shouted, and dropped me.

My fall to the ground hurt, but I didn't stop to think about my bruises. I ran as fast as I could to get away.

Luckily, there was a tree nearby with one of

those holes that I'd discovered earlier. I darted into the hole and waited.

Of course, the children all came running after me.

A hand reached into the hole. I was tempted to give another bite, but I resisted. Instead, I squeezed into the furthest corner of the dark hole and held still. If I was very quiet, maybe they would all get bored and go away.

"Get a stick!" a boy shouted. "Poke him out."

I shuddered at the thought of a stick invading my hiding place. Then I heard another voice. "I just felt a drop of rain."

"It's not raining. You're crazy."

"No, I felt it too," said someone else.

"We'd better go home before the rain really starts coming down."

"Aw. Who's afraid of a little rain?" another boy asked.

Suddenly I could hear the sound of all the children running off. I waited a moment and then peeked out of my hole. A pair of squirrels came scampering past on the ground. I knew that they were some of Lexi's brothers or cousins. But before I could introduce myself, the squirrels were chasing each other halfway up a tree.

Drops of water were falling from the sky now. I guessed that's what the children called *rain*. The sky was darker and the tree branches were swaying in the wind. I crawled back inside the tree hole and waited to see what would happen next.

CHAPTER EIGHT

Water from Above

I pushed deep into the tree hole, but the water seemed to follow me. In fact, the water was coming through the same hole in the ground that I had used to get in. I found some leaves inside the hole and pushed them toward the opening. It kept more water from getting into my hiding place, but it also cut off my air supply. It was stuffy inside the tree.

After a little while, I began to feel very

hungry. But when I pushed the leaves away from the opening in hopes of going out, the water was still pouring down, so I quickly put my head back inside the hole. My hungry stomach made me think about the pellets I ate in my cage. During my short time in the park, I had begun to think of pellets with disgust. But if only I could have a few of them now! I was starving for any kind of food.

Once as I looked out, I could see a sudden flash of light followed by a terrifying bang. And just as I had begun longing for pellets, I started wishing for the quiet safety of my cage. But gradually, I realized that the light and noise weren't going to harm me. And finally, I did the only thing a sensible guinea pig could do in the situation. I fell asleep.

When I woke and opened my hole once

again, the water had finally stopped falling. The flashes had stopped and the big daytime light had not yet been turned on. I suppose the smart thing to do would have been to leave the hole open and get some fresh air while I continued sleeping. But I felt too restless to stay put.

Slowly and softly, I started off. I knew there was no way Robbie would be outdoors at this hour. So my plan was to get back to Lexi and warn him about the play area that was going to destroy his home.

The ground around me was soft and muddy from all the water that had poured down. It wasn't the ideal condition for walking, especially since my eyesight is not good in the dark. Once I rushed joyfully toward what looked like another guinea pig, only to discover that it was a small hard rock. I was very disappointed.

Not long afterward, I thought I smelled something good to eat. Suddenly a voice called out. "Don't touch this food. It belongs to me. I saw it first."

I squinted into the darkness and saw that just inches away, there was a huge, dark creature. Quickly, I moved so that the rock—which only moments before I had hoped was another guinea pig—was between me and this big, chewing animal. I watched as she used her strong claws to rip open a bag of food. Even in the dark, I could recognize an apple lying next to the creature, as well as something round and white. The creature took the white thing and washed it in a nearby puddle.

"What are you?" I asked timidly.

"My name is Sewer Drain. I'm a raccoon," she replied through a mouthful of food.

A raccoon! I'd never heard of a raccoon before. There were none at Casey's Pet Shop. She looked big enough to make a meal of me.

As if reading my thoughts, Sewer Drain spoke again. "What are you? And are you good to eat?"

"No. No. No," I said, trying to think of something more convincing to say. Suddenly, I remembered what Lexi had said about the apple when we had shared it earlier in the day.

"I'm a guinea pig. My name's PeeWee and I'm sour, sour, sour. You wouldn't like my taste at all."

"Guinea pig?" Sewer Drain asked. "I've never seen your kind before." She grunted and kept chewing her meal. I realized that the only reason we could have this conversation was that she was busy with the food in front of her. Otherwise, she would have bit into me first and asked questions afterward. Only then, I wouldn't have been in any shape to come up with answers.

"Tell me, Sue," I said, trying to sound a little more confident, "where do you live?"

"In a sewer drain, of course," she said. "You aren't very smart, are you?"

"I guess I'm not as smart as you," I admitted, although I did have my doubts about that. "I'm new here. Are there many other raccoons around?"

"There are at least a dozen," she responded, gobbling up the apple in two enormous bites.

"Well, you be sure and tell them that guinea pigs are sour," I reminded her.

"Sour," Sue repeated. "I don't like sour. I like sweet. I like corn. I like carrots. I like sandwiches. I like garbage."

"Well, Sue, you're in luck then," I told her. "There's loads of garbage in the park."

"I know that," she agreed, washing her paws in the puddle.

"I think there's a lot of garbage over that way," I told her, and pointed off in the distance, far from the direction I had come.

"Good," Sue said. She turned and moved slowly and quietly away. Even in the dark, I could see that she had a fine thick tail. Why was it that all the animals I met had such big tails when guinea pigs had only little stubs?

I hoped I'd never meet Sewer Drain again. But if I did, I hoped she would remember just one thing: Guinea pigs are sour.

After my close escape, I thought I'd better return to my tree. But it was so dark that I couldn't locate it. Digging a new burrow was hard now that the ground was so muddy. But eventually, I was safe inside the ground again.

I needed a good night's sleep. Tomorrow I would turn back and find Lexi. It was important that he hear what I'd read in the newspaper.

CHAPTER NINE

Water Down Below

The sky was just turning light again when I woke. I climbed out of my burrow and I looked down at myself. My beautiful fur was matted with mud from my temporary home. Grooming myself was hard work.

I rolled in the wet grass at my feet. That loosened some of the mud, but I was still filthy. Then I had an idea. It was early and, although I could hear some birds singing in the trees above me, there were no people in sight. I ran in the direction of the lake. I remembered that every evening before he went to bed, Robbie took a bath. I could take a bath in the lake!

At the water's edge, I stood for a moment looking at it all. I felt that I was looking at all the water in the world. I never knew that there could be so much. Bravely, I put one paw in. The water was icy, but when I took my paw out, I could see that it had become perfectly clean. So I took a deep breath and forced myself to walk into that freezing water. I shivered at first, but gradually, I didn't feel the cold any more. I moved my paws and actually felt myself floating in the water. It was fun.

Remembering all of Lexi's warnings, I decided to get back to land. I shook myself all over and some of the water flew off my fur. The rest would soon dry from the sun.

I hadn't been in the water long, but already I could see a change in the park. More birds were singing, squirrels were darting about, and a few humans were walking their dogs or running along the paths.

I hid behind a thick bush and found a leaf to nibble on. It was a bitter breakfast, but better than nothing in my empty stomach. A squirrel raced past me.

"Hello," I called. "Who are you? Are you related to Lexi?"

"Fifty-nine," the squirrel shouted, but he kept on running.

A second squirrel was close on his heels. "Who are you?" I yelled.

"Fifty-two," the squirrel responded, but like

the first one, he was gone before I had a chance to respond.

At first I wondered what those numbers meant. Then I remembered what Lexi had told me. I had just met two of his relatives who were named after street numbers. I wondered if their trees were in danger of being cut down. I knew I should hurry on and find Lexi. He needed to know about the plans for the new playground.

My travels toward his tree were pretty eventful. Two humans whizzed by me on strangely familiar devices with big wheels. I jumped out of their way and, as I caught my breath, I realized what I'd just seen. Those were bicycles. Robbie had a bicycle that stood in the hallway of his apartment. But I'd never seen it in use and I hadn't realized that it would be able to move so quickly.

As I stood hiding behind a rock, I saw a squirrel busily eating a nut. Since he wasn't dashing up a tree, I thought I'd have a better chance at starting a conversation. "Hello," I called to him. "You must be a relative of my friend Lexi."

The squirrel looked up from his snack. "I'm his cousin. I'm Seventy-one." He finished his nut and then added, "That's my name, not my age."

"I'm PeeWee. I'm a guinea pig. And yesterday I read a story in the newspaper about—"

Before I could say another word, Seventy-one was gone like the nut he had been eating.

Suddenly, and quite unexpectedly, I felt

myself being lifted into the air. For a second, I thought I had been picked up by a human. But when I twisted my head, I saw the eyes and beak of a huge bird.

"Let me go!" I squeaked in a weak voice, terrified of my captor.

The bird ignored me and, what's worse, he began to fly higher and higher.

I squirmed about in his talons as best I

could, but he held me tight. When I looked down, everything looked small and far away. I closed my eyes with fright. But then I opened them again and saw that I was above the treetops, higher than Lexi had ever gone.

Below me I saw something shining brightly. It was the lake. I knew that this was my only chance. I moved my head and took a fierce bite of the bird's leg. I guess I surprised him, because he let go of me and I began falling, falling, falling.

. Had I landed on the ground, my story would be over. But because we had been flying over the lake, I landed with a tremendous splash in the water. My eyes and mouth filled with the lake water. I raised my head, spit out the water, and blinked my eyes so I could see. And then I swam toward the shore.

"It's a water rat!" I heard someone scream. But luckily, I made it safely to a crevice of a nearby tree. I sat there catching my breath for several minutes. What an adventure I would have to report to Lexi—if I ever made it back to Lexi, I thought.

I remained in hiding for quite a long while. I had forgotten, once again, that life outside a cage was full of dangers. From one moment to the next, anything could happen to me. But as soon as I caught my breath and dried up a bit from my second bath of the morning, I began to feel better. It was my own fault. Lexi had warned me to watch where I was going.

As I retraced the route I had taken earlier, I saw a group of pigeons flocking around a bench. I knew I didn't have to worry about pigeons. But a human was throwing something to them and I didn't want her to see me. Cautiously, I crept past. Suddenly, I felt myself hit by something small and hard. It was a nut that the human was throwing to the birds. I picked it up with my teeth and then hid under the bench as I ate it. If only I could manage to take some of these nuts to Lexi. Boldly, I snatched a couple more from the ground, just as a pigeon was about to pounce on them.

"Food. Food," he grumbled, but there were so many nuts around that he had no reason to complain.

I kept the nuts gently inside my mouth so I could bring them to Lexi. I wished I could take still more, but my mouth was not large enough.

I ran through the longer grass and weeds, hoping that I was going in the right direction.

And finally, my efforts were rewarded. A voice called out to me.

"So, you're back again!"

"Lexi!" I called, spitting out the nuts that I had been carrying. "I brought you a couple of nuts."

"Why, so you have! Peanuts," Lexi exclaimed delightedly.

"I wanted to bring more, but I couldn't carry them," I said apologetically.

"*A nut in the jaw is worth two in the paw*," Lexi responded.

"I have something very important to tell you," I said. "I read a newspaper story about a new play area for children that's going to be built right here. I'm pretty sure your tree is going to be cut down. You've got to find a new home and move all of your nuts."

"It doesn't make sense," Lexi said. "Squirrels have been climbing trees since time began. If children need something to do, why don't they climb the trees too?"

"Children do climb trees. But they like to do other things too. Besides, it's already been decided. The trees are coming down. So if you want to rescue your nuts, you'd better get them now, before it's too late."

"There have been lots of men walking about

here lately," Lexi admitted. "I didn't take much notice. In fact, I was dumb enough to be proud when they pointed to my tree," he said. "I thought they were noticing what a wonderful tree I'd selected for my home."

Lexi stopped talking and scampered up his tree. He returned a moment later with his mouth full of nuts. I watched as he ran off with them. I was tired after my morning's adventures, so I sat under a nearby bush and waited to see what was going to happen next.

"I found a new home," a voice said in my ear. I'd been asleep, but Lexi had spotted me and come to give me the news.

"Where is it?" I asked.

"It's about five hundred paws away," he told me.

"Is that far?" I wondered aloud.

"Far enough away to be safe," he said. "But near enough to feel like I'm still on my own turf. I'm sure glad that you warned me so I can take all the nuts I've stored away. It would be a terrible waste to lose them all."

"The saddest thing is to lose a home," I told him, thinking about Robbie. "But it's good to find another home that you like. That's the way I feel about this park."

Lexi looked at me and scratched himself thoughtfully. "PeeWee," he said, "you may not have a tail and you may not be much of a climber, but you have a good head. *A good head is worth two tails,*" he observed.

CHAPTER TEN
Life in the Park

By dark, Lexi had transferred all of his possessions to his new home. Since I own nothing, I
was amazed at how much Lexi had. I helped as
well as I could by dragging a piece of cloth
and later by carrying one or two nuts. I wish I
could have helped him more, but I moved so
slowly that Lexi made a dozen trips in the time
it took me to complete just one.

Other squirrels were busy rushing about and moving their possessions too. Two of the doomed trees were the homes of families with very young squirrels. Their mothers carried them to safety. We all knew that without enough warning, those little squirrels would not have survived when their homes were destroyed.

"How did you manage to warn all your relatives?" I asked Lexi when I saw all the activity around us. By now I'd been in the park long enough to realize that there were as many squirrels running up and down the trees as there were people walking around during daylight.

"I told every squirrel I saw to tell every squirrel they saw to tell every squirrel they saw to tell every squirrel they saw to tell—"

"Stop," I said. "I understand."

"Anyhow, they all heard your story. And they all admitted that they'd seen too many men walking around here lately." Lexi looked at me. "There's just one thing I've been wondering about," he said.

"What's that?" I asked.

"Tell me again, how did you discover that these trees were going to be cut down?"

"It's very simple," I explained. "When I was looking for Robbie, I found a newspaper. I read all about the plan for the new play area in the paper."

"That's what I thought you said," Lexi responded. "But how did you know how to read?"

"My mother taught me," I told him proudly.

"You actually know how to read?" Lexi asked me with amazement. "I've never heard of an animal who could read."

"Well, I can do it. I always thought reading would be fun. But I didn't get any pleasure from reading that newspaper. Half of it was filled with words that held no meaning whatsoever. And the other half had bad news that upset me."

"I've been watching people read ever since I was a young squirrel," Lexi said. "They read newspapers and magazines. They read big books and small books. And it holds their attention for hours. It must make sense and it must be fun."

"Human beings are strange," I pointed out.

"You're right about that," Lexi agreed. "But

I think you're wrong about reading. After all, if you hadn't read about the trees being cut down, who knows how many squirrels would have been homeless or even killed when their trees fell down."

I nodded. There was some truth in what Lexi said.

"Wait here," he told me. I watched as Lexi raced up his new tree to his nest at the very top. I thought I'd seen everything he owned during the move. But somehow, I'd missed seeing one thing. A moment later, Lexi ran down the tree holding a small book inside his mouth.

"I found this many months ago," he said. "I've kept it just because I kept it. I couldn't read it. I couldn't eat it. But still I kept it. And now I know why. You can read it to me."

I looked at the cover of the book: *The Best-Loved Poems of the English Language.*

"Those words don't make sense," I pointed out.

"Never mind," said Lexi. "Open it up and read it aloud. Maybe it will be better inside."

I turned the pages with my paws. These are the words I read:

> *Summer is y-comen in,*
> *Loude sing, cuckoo!*
> *Groweth seed and bloweth meed*
> *And spring'th the woode now—*
> *Sing cuckoo!*

"What does it mean?" I asked Lexi.

"I don't know. But it has a fine sound. Go on. Read some more."

I read the whole poem twice over. Lexi repeated the words.

I listened to him and I said, "You know, I think I understand them after all. Summer is here. And we're happy. The birds are singing."

"That's right," agreed Lexi. "Cuckoos are birds. And they're singing loudly." I turned the pages with my paws and read another poem. And then another and another.

I wandered lonely as a cloud
That floats on high o'er vales and hills,
When all at once I saw a crowd,
A host of golden daffodils;
Beside the lake, beneath the trees
Fluttering and dancing in the breeze.

For once, Lexi forgot about his stomach and I forgot about mine. I looked up and saw that all around us were sitting other animals, listening.

"Don't stop," said a pigeon. "More. More."

Though my tongue was tired and thirsty, my head was full of wonderful words and messages. There *was* pleasure in reading. It was not just for me, the reader, but for everyone who heard me say the words.

After that, Lexi and the other squirrels were on the lookout for any books that human beings had abandoned in the park. The birds couldn't carry books, but they reported whenever they saw one lying on the grass or on a park bench. Soon Lexi had to find still another tree hole just for storing the books.

Each evening, after the park emptied out, we gathered together. I got to meet many of Lexi's brothers and sisters, as well as other kinds of animals who wanted to listen to me read. To my horror, one evening the huge bird who had tried to carry me away came with his mate. I shivered with fear when I looked up from my reading and saw him in my audience. But afterward, he thanked me for the experience of listening to the words. I knew I never had to fear him again.

Just as Lexi marveled at my reading ability, I felt great awe that he knew so much about living in the park. I am sure I would never have managed without him. Not only did he rescue me from danger more than once, but he continued to teach me many wise sayings so that I could take control of my own life. Things like *Don't count your nuts before they are shelled*, and *Don't cry over a rotten nut*. He talked a lot about nuts, but I quickly learned that these lessons applied to more than just food.

CHAPTER ELEVEN

Robbie

Lexi and I watched from the distance as the work began on the children's play area. Even though he was safely settled in a new tree, it was a sad moment for Lexi to see his old home destroyed. The noise of the construction work was horrible, so we didn't stay long. We were lucky that the park was so large that we could run away and ignore what was happening in that small section.

I loved my new life in the park with its grasses, bushes, space, and color. I was thriving on the delicious and varied sources of food. I'd made many, many new friends—too many to count. Just as important, I'd become skilled at hiding from humans who were not my friends. I'd never be able to run as fast as Lexi and the other squirrels. I'd never be able to climb a tree. But I'd learned how to move quickly by guinea pig standards. I'd learned to dart from one direction to another, which confused anyone who tried to catch me. In fact, it was rare for any human to ever catch a glimpse of me nowadays. And nothing was more fun than my reading sessions with the park creatures listening to me.

I spent my nights in a comfortable tree hole that Lexi had discovered for me. The tree was enormous and although the entrance was very small, the space inside was twice the size of any I'd discovered on my own. I had room to store food and dry leaves to keep me cozy. Best of all, the tree was very near to the one where Lexi lived, and so we were neighbors.

But one thing bothered me every day: my thoughts of my friend Robbie. Not only did he not get a dog for his birthday, he didn't even have a guinea pig anymore. Was he missing me? Who could he talk to if I wasn't there for him?

"Nonsense!" Lexi said to me when I told him how I felt. *"Out of sight, out of mind.* That kid isn't worrying about you, so why are you worrying about him?"

This was one time when I was sure Lexi was wrong, even though he was so wise about so many other things. After all, he'd never even met Robbie! How could he be so certain about how Robbie would behave?

I still watched for Robbie as I ran around the park. And I described him over and over again to any creature who would listen to me. There was a whole network of birds and squirrels who had promised to look for him. They said they'd tell me if they ever saw him. Maybe Robbie will come to the new play area when it's completed, I told myself hopefully.

One day, about six weeks after I arrived in the park, Lexi poked his head into my little home and woke me up.

"I think I've found your Robbie," he reported.

"What?" I asked, rubbing the sleep from my eyes with my paws.

"I know I told you that all these children

playing in the park look alike, but not only does this boy have spots on his face, I heard someone calling him by name."

"Where is he?" I asked excitedly.

"He's down near the lake. He was sitting on one of the park benches a few minutes ago. He may still be there," Lexi said.

"I must go at once before he's gone," I said, darting off quickly.

"Wait. There's something else I have to tell you. . . ." Lexi called after me.

"Not now. I don't have time. Tell me later," I shouted back to him.

Because of all the exercise I'd had in recent weeks, I could move at twice the speed I used to. So it didn't take nearly as long for me to reach the benches near the lake as you might think.

Sure enough, I spotted Robbie. He was sitting with another boy and they were eating sandwiches. I ran toward them until I noticed that resting at their feet was a dog.

The dog was on a leash that was attached to the back of the park bench. Still, I'd learned never to trust a dog. So instead of running up to Robbie, as I would have liked to do, I

backed up. I hid under a nearby bush waiting till the boy took his dog away.

The boy was talking to Robbie. Even though his mouth was full of food, I could make out his words. "You really are lucky," he said.

"You're right, Evan," Robbie said. "It all turned out great. But who would've believed it?"

"When did your mom give in?" Evan asked.

"Well, you know I got a guinea pig for my birthday?" Robbie said. The boy nodded and so did I. Robbie was talking about me. I knew he hadn't forgotten me. Lexi was wrong.

"He was a neat pet," Robbie said. "I called him PeeWee because he was small, but even though he was little, he was great."

I groomed myself as I stood hiding behind the bush. By taking regular baths in the lake,

I managed to avoid getting fleas. (I hadn't yet succeeded in convincing Lexi that if he took a few baths, he wouldn't have to scratch himself all the time!) I wanted Robbie to think that I was as handsome as ever.

Robbie kept on talking. "Well, one evening I had a sleepover at my friend Greg's house. And when I came home, PeeWee was gone."

"Where did he go?" Evan asked.

"I don't know. The cage door was open, so I thought he must be somewhere in my bedroom. I looked everywhere. I took every book off the bookshelf. I took every single thing out of my closet."

"And you couldn't find him?"

"Nowhere. Not in my room. Not in the whole apartment."

"Gee. Then what?" asked Evan.

"Well," Robbie said. "Don't tell anyone, okay? But I cried a lot. I worried that PeeWee was lost somewhere in the apartment. And I worried that he'd get hungry. So I sprinkled his pellet food all over, inside all the closets, in the cupboards where my mother stored her pots and canned food. Everywhere."

"I would have cried too," Evan admitted. "And you never found him, did you?"

"Never. My dad said he must have left the apartment building. Maybe he'd gone to live with another family. That really made me stop feeling so sad and made me angry instead. Why would PeeWee want to live with someone else? I thought he liked me."

"I did. I do," I called out and was just about to come out from my hiding place when Robbie said something else.

"Anyhow, after about a week, my mother said, 'All right. Stop making such a fuss about that old rodent.' She always hated PeeWee. She said he reminded her of a hairy rat. And then she said, 'We'll get you a dog.' And that's how I got Dakota."

From my hiding place, I watched as Robbie bent down and petted the dog at his feet. The dog turned his head and licked Robbie's hand.

I was stunned. That dog belonged to Robbie, not to his friend. Robbie didn't need me anymore. He had a new pet. He'd finally gotten the dog he'd dreamed of owning.

"I wonder what happened to your guinea pig?" Evan said.

Robbie shrugged his shoulders. "I just hope wherever he is, he's okay," he said. "He was a neat pet but he was driving my mother insane. Maybe he found a new home where the mother doesn't scream whenever she sees him."

"Grown-ups are funny," Evan said. "My dad is terrified of snakes. I brought Cleopatra, my class snake, home over the Easter holidays and he almost had a heart attack."

"The snake?" asked Robbie.

"No. No. My dad," said Evan.

The two boys stood up and the dog, Dakota, jumped to his feet too. Robbie took the leash in his hand.

"Race you to the fountain," he said to his friend.

And suddenly they were all off and running, as fast as Lexi goes. Faster than I could ever dream of going.

I sat in my hiding place and thought about all I'd heard. I couldn't believe it, but Lexi had been right after all. Robbie didn't need me.

Slowly, I made my way back to my home in the tree. I crawled inside and hid myself under the leaves.

"PeeWee," a voice called to me. It was Lexi.

I didn't feel like responding. But then I felt his paw poking me.

"Come on out," he said.

Reluctantly, I left my hole.

"Look at what I've found for you," said Lexi. He pushed an apple core toward me. "I remembered how much you liked this."

Good old Lexi, I thought as I looked at the fruit he'd brought me.

"Did you find your Robbie?" Lexi asked.

"Yes," I said. "He's got a dog now. A big dog."

"I know," Lexi said to me. "I saw him."

I walked over to the apple core and took a small nibble. It suddenly occurred to me that I'd never tasted any apple before I came to the park. I'd never tasted anything except pellets. I'd never done very much of anything living inside that small cage of mine.

"I just realized something important," I told Lexi. "Robbie is very happy with his dog. He got what he always wanted, so he doesn't need me anymore. But I'm really glad. You know why? Because at the same time, I got what I didn't even know I wanted. I've got freedom and friendship. My life here in the park is better than anything I could ever have dreamed of wanting."

I pushed the apple toward Lexi. "Come over here," I invited him. "Share this with me. You'll like it. It's very sweet."

About the Author and Illustrator

Johanna Hurwitz was born and raised in New York City. A former children's librarian, she is now the award-winning author of many popular books for young readers, including *Class Clown, Rip-Roaring Russell, Baseball Fever,* and *Faraway Summer.* The recipient of a number of child-chosen state awards, she visits schools around the country to speak to students, teachers and parents about reading and writing. She lives in both Great Neck, New York, and Wilmington, Vermont.

Patience Brewster has illustrated more than thirty books, including *Bear's Christmas Surprise* by Elizabeth Winthrop and *Queen of May* by Steven Kroll. She lives in Skaneateles, New York.